The Play

Written by
Stephen Rickard

I am a cowboy.
I am in the play.

I am a fairy.
I am in the play.

I am a lion.
I am in the play.

I am a princess.
I am in the play.

I am a strongman.
I am in the play.

I am a pirate.
I am in the play.

I am a rabbit.
I am in the play.

I am a clown.
I am in the play.

I am a doctor.
I am in the play.

I am a fireman.
I am in the play.

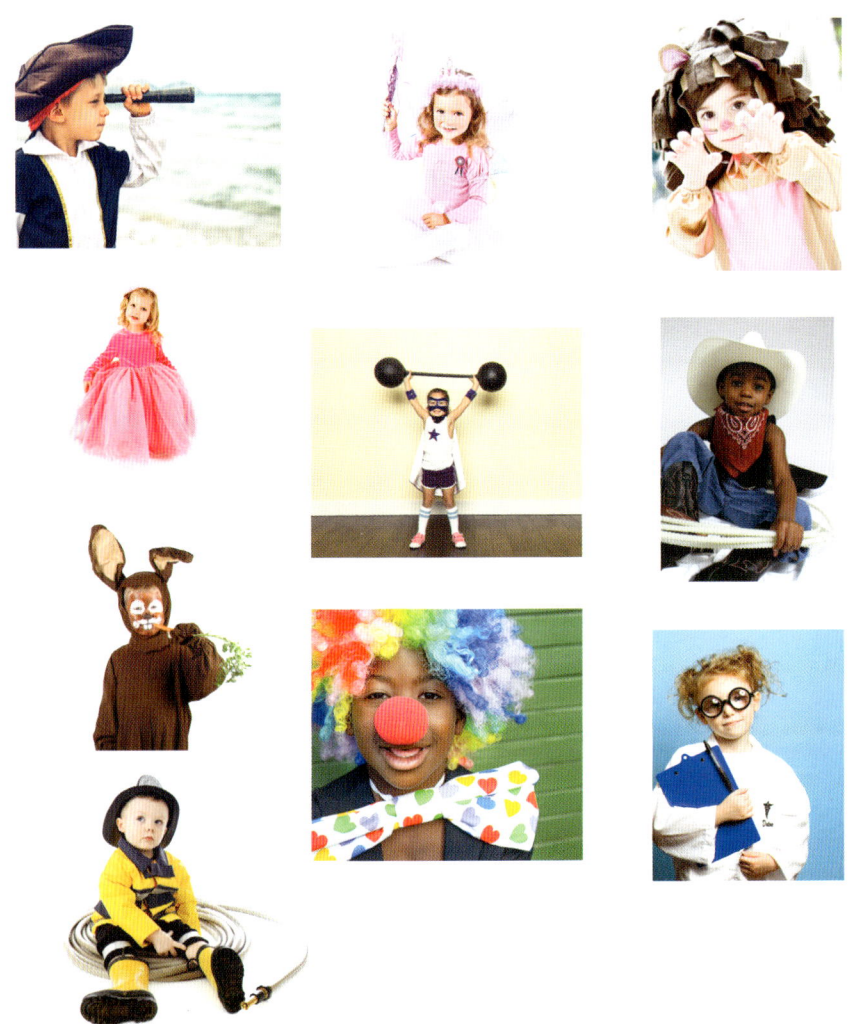

We are in the play.